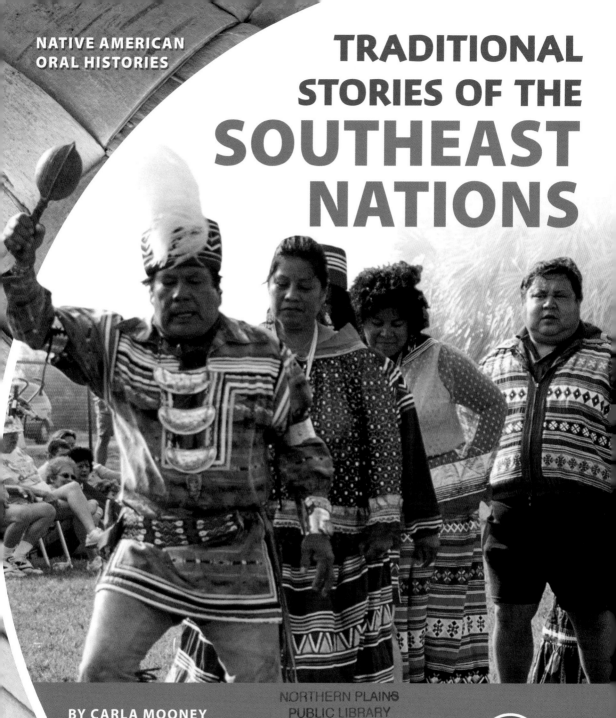

TRADITIONAL STORIES OF THE SOUTHEAST NATIONS

BY CARLA MOONEY

CONTENT CONSULTANT
Frances Kay Holmes, PhD
Assistant Professor, Native American and Indigenous Studies
Fort Lewis College

Core Library

An Imprint of Abdo Publishing
abdopublishing.com

Cover image: Seminole dancers perform a traditional
stomp dance.

abdopublishing.com

Published by Abdo Publishing, a division of ABDO, PO Box 398166,
Minneapolis, Minnesota 55439. Copyright © 2018 by Abdo Consulting
Group, Inc. International copyrights reserved in all countries. No part of this
book may be reproduced in any form without written permission from the
publisher. Core Library™ is a trademark and logo of Abdo Publishing.

Printed in the United States of America, North Mankato, Minnesota
032017
092017

THIS BOOK CONTAINS
RECYCLED MATERIALS

Cover Photo: Marilyn Angel Wynn/NativeStock
Interior Photos: Marilyn Angel Wynn/NativeStock, 1; Lou Krasky/AP Images, 4–5; Joseph Sohm/
Shutterstock Images, 7; Shutterstock Images, 8; John Fitzhugh/Sun Herald/AP Images, 11, 45;
Jukka Risikko/Shutterstock Images, 14–15, 43; Otis Imboden/National Geographic/Getty Images,
16; Visual Studies Workshop/Archive Photos/Getty Images, 19; Jorge R. Gonzalez/Shutterstock
Images, 22–23; Willard R. Culver/National Geographic/Getty Images, 25; iStockphoto, 28–29;
Picture History/Newscom, 34–35; Red Line Editorial, 36; John Tlumacki/The Boston Globe/Getty
Images, 38–39

Editor: Arnold Ringstad
Imprint Designer: Maggie Villaume
Series Design Direction: Ryan Gale

Publisher's Cataloging-in-Publication Data

Names: Mooney, Carla, author.
Title: Traditional stories of the Southeast nations / by Carla Mooney.
Description: Minneapolis, MN : Abdo Publishing, 2018. | Series: Native American
    oral histories | Includes bibliographical references and index.
Identifiers: LCCN 2017930252 | ISBN 9781532111761 (lib. bdg.) |
    ISBN 9781680789614 (ebook)
Subjects: LCSH: Indians of North America--Juvenile literature. | Indians of North
    America--Social life and customs--Juvenile literature. | Indian mythology--
    North America--Juvenile literature. | Indians of North America--Folklore--
    Juvenile literature.
Classification: DDC 979--dc23
    LC record available at http://lccn.loc.gov/2017930252

CONTENTS

CHAPTER ONE
**Native American Nations
of the Southeast** **4**

CHAPTER TWO
Stealing Fire **14**

CHAPTER THREE
Linked to the Land **22**

CHAPTER FOUR
Trickster Tales **28**

CHAPTER FIVE
**The Lasting Impact
of Oral Histories** **34**

Story Summaries **42**

Stop and Think **44**

Glossary **46**

Learn More **47**

Index **48**

About the Author **48**

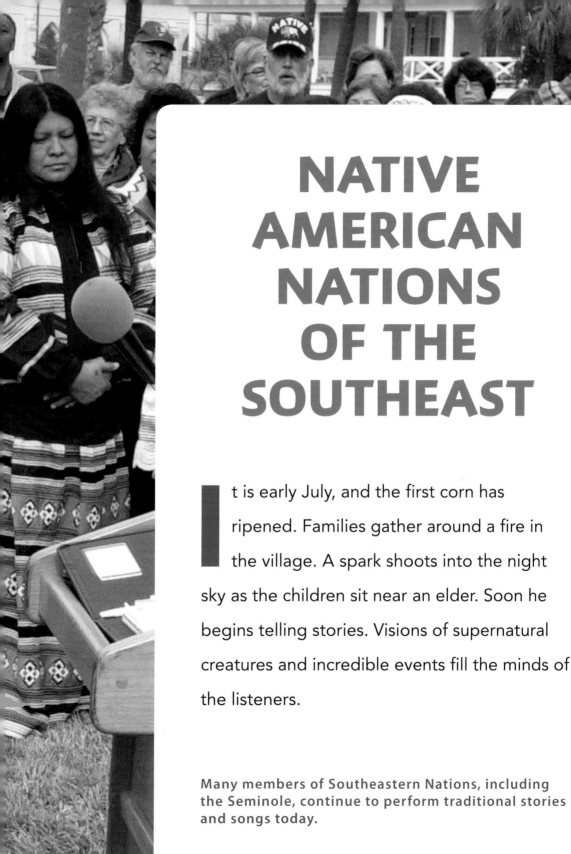

NATIVE AMERICAN NATIONS OF THE SOUTHEAST

It is early July, and the first corn has ripened. Families gather around a fire in the village. A spark shoots into the night sky as the children sit near an elder. Soon he begins telling stories. Visions of supernatural creatures and incredible events fill the minds of the listeners.

Many members of Southeastern Nations, including the Seminole, continue to perform traditional stories and songs today.

Native American Nations have long lived in the Southeastern United States. Archaeologists have found evidence of settlements dating back more than 18,000 years. Tribes settled across an area that stretched across the present-day states of Louisiana, Mississippi, Tennessee, Alabama, Florida, Georgia, South Carolina, North Carolina, and Virginia. The land has mountains, forests, swamps, grasslands, and rivers. Major tribes in the Southeast include the Cherokee, Chickasaw, Choctaw, Creek, Natchez, and Seminole.

LIVING IN VILLAGES

Most of the tribes in the Southeast lived in villages. Often they built these villages near rivers. The central point of each village was its plaza. People gathered at the plaza for special events, dancing, and games. The village's council house, where ceremonies were held, often stood in the plaza.

Water played a central role in the lives of Southeastern tribes.

MAP OF SOUTHEASTERN NATIONS

This map shows the modern locations of Southeastern Nations. Several Native American tribes have long lived in the Southeastern United States. How do you think the tribes' environments affected their way of life? How might that have had an impact on their oral traditions?

Family homes surrounded the village's central plaza. The people built homes using local materials. The Cherokee people lived in log and mud houses. The Creek people built houses shingled with wood or grass. In Florida, the Seminole people lived in houses called chickees. They built these homes on stilts to raise them above the water level. The chickees had no sides, a wooden floor, and a thatched roof. Farming fields encircled each village.

BELIEFS AND STORYTELLING

Many people of the Southeastern tribes believe that they are linked to the world around them. For them it has always been important to stay in harmony with nature. People saw everything in nature as having a spirit, including animals, plants, and trees. Respecting nature was an important part of their connection with these spirits.

Before the Europeans arrived in America, Native Americans in the Southeast did not use a written language. Instead, they passed

SACRED STORIES

Some stories are considered sacred. In special ceremonies, people reenact such traditional stories. Many tribes also believed that sacred stories could only be told at certain times, like on a winter night. Only certain people, such as spiritual leaders, could tell these stories.

Choctaw council leader Terry Ladnier, *left*, passes along traditions to younger generations at a 2014 ceremony.

on their history, culture, and beliefs through spoken language and storytelling.

Like many other cultures, the tribes of the Southeast talked about their world through storytelling. They used stories to explain nature and how the world was created. Creation stories told of the origin of man.

Other stories explained natural phenomena. The people also had stories about the environment and problems facing their tribes.

The Southeastern Nations have used and continue to use stories to record their history and culture. Some stories explain tribal customs and religious ceremonies. Other stories teach the values and ideals that are important to a tribe. The people passed these stories down from generation to generation. Much of what people know today about the tribes of the Southeast comes from studying these oral stories. Today, Native Americans from Southeastern Nations still tell many stories. For these Native American Nations, storytelling provides a connection to their ancestors.

STRAIGHT TO THE
SOURCE

Barbara Braveboy-Locklear is a Lumbee storyteller. In an interview, she talked about the role of stories:

The art of storytelling is a much-respected position among tribes and is usually reserved for the elders. The distinctive work of the grandparents is that of acquainting the children with the traditions and beliefs of the nation. It is reserved for them to repeat the time-hallowed tales with dignity and authority, so as to lead the child into the inheritance of the stored-up wisdom and experience of the race. Today, though storytelling faces a lot of competition from outside sources, folklore remains alive in the homes of families who have valued it deeply. . . . The stories help keep the American Indian culture alive, which helps to keep the history and culture from being diluted or destroyed in America's "melting pot."

Source: "Lumbee in Touch with the Earth." *Storytelling of the North Carolina Native Americans*. Sunsite, December 8, 1998. Web. Accessed January 6, 2017.

Changing Minds

The author of this passage is using evidence to support a point. Write a paragraph describing the point the author is making. Then write down two or three pieces of evidence the author uses to make the point.

CHAPTER
TWO

STEALING FIRE

Native peoples use creation stories to explain how the world came to be. Grandmother Spider is an important figure in the creation stories of many Native American cultures, including those in the Southeast.

In some traditions, Grandmother Spider creates the stars in the sky. In other stories, Grandmother Spider creates man. The following Choctaw creation story tells how Grandmother Spider stole fire. She then brought it to humans so that they could use it to light up the world and improve their daily lives.

The making of the night sky is a common theme in creation stories.

The story of Grandmother Spider involves fire. Open flames remain important in Southeast Nations' cooking today.

GRANDMOTHER SPIDER STEALS THE FIRE

In the beginning, the world was dark. There was no sun,

no moon, and no stars. The people and animals could

not see anything, so they moved by feeling their way around. They had no fire to cook their food. The people and animals had a big meeting. Someone spoke of people in the east who had fire to give them light and warmth. They were too greedy to share the fire.

Many animals tried to steal the fire. Each returned empty-handed. The animals and people despaired. Who could steal the fire? Tiny

Grandmother Spider volunteered. The people did not think she would succeed. But they agreed to let her try. Grandmother Spider went to a stream where she found clay. Using her eight legs, she created a tiny clay container. She also made a lid with a tiny notch for air. She put the container on her back. Then she spun a web all the way to the east. She walked on the web until she came to the fire. She was so small, the people from the east did not see her. Grandmother Spider took a tiny piece of fire. She put it into the clay container. Then she walked back along the web. When she returned, the people could not see the fire and thought she had failed. But when Grandmother Spider lifted the lid from the pot, the fire flamed up into the air.

Who would get the fire? The animals were afraid of it. The birds did not want it. The insects also stayed far from it. Finally, the humans volunteered to take the fire. Grandmother Spider taught the people how to feed the fire wood to keep it burning. She taught them how to keep it safe in a circle of stone. She taught the humans

Choctaw women weave baskets in Oklahoma in the early 1900s.

about pottery made of clay and fire. She also taught them about weaving and spinning.

GIVER OF LIFE

The story of Grandmother Spider shows the importance of women in Choctaw culture. In the story, Grandmother

Spider is a wise, old female character. She earns the respect of the other animals and humans. She teaches humans how to control and use fire.

Like Grandmother Spider, Choctaw women are the givers and supporters of life. One of the Choctaw people's traditional values is a great respect for women. They honor women as the head of every family. Choctaw people trace their ancestry through their mothers.

Choctaw women gave life by bearing children. They also worked hard to support their families. They traditionally produced most of the food their families ate. The women were in charge

CLAY POTTERY

Native people in the Southeast have made clay pottery for at least 5,000 years. Clay is found along the region's streams and hillsides. The people used clay pots for cooking and eating. The Choctaw people made two main types of pots. Shoti cooking pots were plain. Ampo eating bowls were polished and decorated. One type of design was made by scraping a comb across the soft clay to create fine parallel lines.

of the fields. They grew corn and other crops. They gathered greens, fruit, vegetables, and nuts from the woods. They prepared the family meals.

The Choctaw women were also artists. They created baskets, textiles, and pottery. Choctaw girls practiced these crafts from a young age. Women remain important in Choctaw society today. The tribe's war dances, unlike those of many other tribes, include not only men but also women.

FURTHER EVIDENCE

Chapter Two includes information about creation stories. Explore the website below to learn more about Native American creation stories. Find a quote from the website that supports the chapter's main point. Does the quote support an existing piece of evidence in the chapter? Or does it add a new piece of evidence?

NATIVE STORYTELLERS CONNECT THE PAST AND FUTURE
abdocorelibrary.com/southeast-nations

CHAPTER THREE

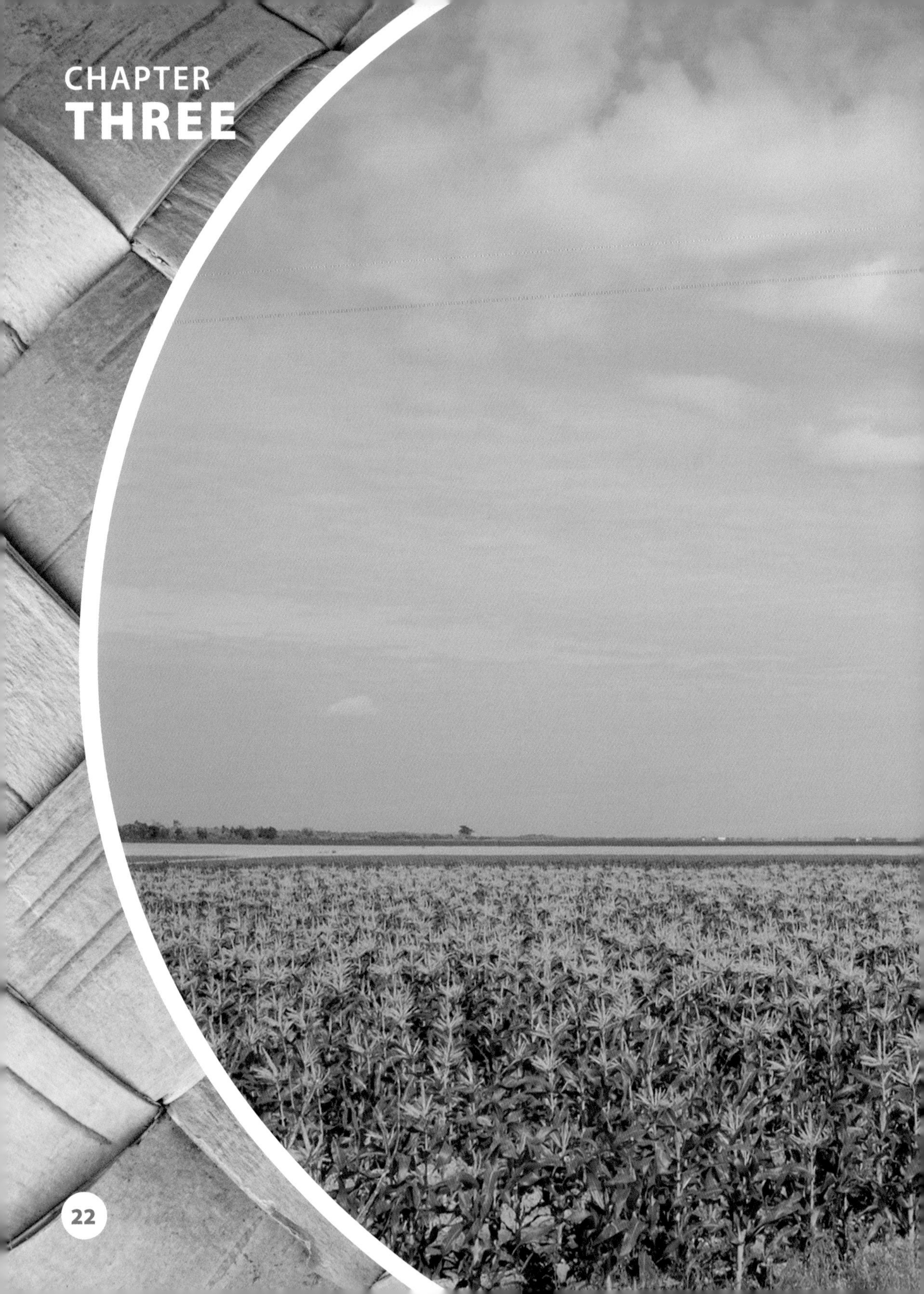

LINKED TO THE LAND

The link between the land and people is a common theme in Native American life. Southeastern Nations farmed on the land's rich soil. For many tribes, corn was the primary crop. It was an important part of their diet.

The Southeastern Nations tell stories about the origin of corn and how it came to humans. Many of the stories feature a corn mother or woman. The following story is from the Natchez. It explains where corn came from and why people must work hard to grow it.

Corn, an important crop to Southeast tribes, is still grown in Florida today.

THE ORIGIN OF CORN

A long time ago, the Corn Woman lived with twin girls. Every day, she went to the storehouse with two empty baskets. When she came out, corn and beans filled the baskets. The curious girls looked into the storehouse. They saw nothing. They wondered where the woman got the food. They decided to spy on the woman the next time she went to the storehouse.

The next time the Corn Woman went to the storehouse, the girls crept after her. They peered through a crack in the door. They watched the Corn Woman put down the basket. She stood over it. She rubbed and shook her

MOUND BUILDING

The Natchez people were known as great mound builders. Beginning around 800 CE, they constructed large piles of earth arranged in particular shapes. Mound building was an expression of the tribe's spiritual beliefs. The earthen mounds served as bases for sacred buildings. By the 1500s CE, the practice of mound building was in decline.

A Seminole woman grinds up corn.

body. Then there was a noise as something fell into the basket. She did this until the basket was filled with corn. She filled a second basket with beans.

The girls ran away. When the Corn Woman made the next meal, the girls refused to eat. The Corn Woman knew that the girls had seen her. She told the girls, "Since you think my food is filthy, you will have to help yourselves from now on."

The Corn Woman told the girls to burn her body and spread the ashes on the ground. The girls did as they were told. When summer came, corn, beans, and pumpkins grew where they had spread the Corn Woman's ashes. The girls tended these crops every day. As they finished each day, they left their hoes stuck in the ground. When they returned the next day, they found their hoes in different places. Someone had hoed more ground. "Let's creep up at night and find out who is doing this," the girls said.

That night, the girls sneaked to the field. They saw the hoes working by themselves. The sight made them laugh out loud. Immediately, the hoes fell to the ground. The hoes did not work again. Since that day, people have had to work hard to tend their fields.

IMPORTANCE OF CORN

The Natchez people originally lived in Mississippi before the US government forced them to move west in the 1800s. The Mississippi land had rich soil and a warm climate. This made it good for growing crops. The Natchez became successful farmers. They grew corn, beans, and squash. Many tribes call these crops the three sisters.

The Natchez and other Southeastern tribes acknowledge the importance of corn by holding special ceremonies. They hold the Green Corn Ceremony in late summer when the corn has ripened. All fires in the community are extinguished, then rekindled. The ceremony involves fasting and dancing.

TRICKSTER TALES

Like many cultures around the world, the Southeastern tribes tell trickster tales. A trickster is a clever animal or person who fools other characters. Tricksters can have positive or negative qualities. Trickster stories are often told to entertain an audience. They can also be used to teach lessons.

In many Southeastern tribes, Rabbit is a trickster figure. Rabbit is typically a lighthearted character. He often behaves inappropriately and is careless. The following story is from the Cherokee. It explains how something in nature became the way that it is.

Rabbits are common animals in the Southeast, and they play roles in many of these Nations' stories.

WHY THE POSSUM'S TAIL IS BARE

Possum had a long, bushy tail. He was very proud of his tail. He combed it every morning. He sang about it at dances. Rabbit was jealous of Possum's tail. He decided to play a trick on Possum.

A great meeting and dance was going to be held. Rabbit asked Possum if he was coming to the dance. Possum said, "I'll only go if I can have a special seat. I have a handsome tail, so I ought to sit where everybody can see me." Rabbit promised he would find Possum a special seat. He also said he would send someone to comb and dress Possum's tail. Possum was very pleased.

Rabbit then went to see Cricket. Cricket was an expert at cutting hair. Rabbit told Cricket to go to Possum's house in the morning. He wanted Cricket to get Possum's tail ready for the dance. Rabbit told Cricket how he wanted Possum's tail styled.

The next morning, Cricket went to Possum's house. He told Possum he had come to help Possum get ready for the dance. Possum stretched on the floor. He closed his eyes. Cricket combed Possum's tail. He wrapped a red string around it to keep the fur smooth until the dance. As he wrapped the string, Cricket cut off the tail's hair. Possum never knew.

That night, Possum went to the dance. Just as Rabbit promised, he saved the best seat for Possum. Possum sat down and waited to dance. When it was his turn, Possum

PERSPECTIVES

THE TRICKSTER TRICKED

Sometimes, the trickster himself is tricked. In one Choctaw story, the trickster Turkey boasted to Terrapin, a turtle, that he was the fastest runner. Terrapin and Turkey agreed to race. Terrapin knew he could not beat Turkey. So he called on his family for help. He placed turtles along the race course, each holding a white feather. The race began, and Turkey sprinted as fast as he could. Terrapin stood still at the starting line. But as Turkey ran, he saw a turtle with a white feather at every turn. He thought Terrapin was running. As Turkey came around the last turn, Terrapin stood at the finish line, waving his white feather.

loosened the red string from his tail. He stepped into the dance circle. The drummers banged their drums. Possum danced and sang. He boasted about his beautiful tail. The animals shouted. Suddenly, Possum realized everyone was laughing at him. He stopped and looked down at his tail. There was no hair on it. It was completely bare. Possum was very upset and embarrassed. He fell over on the ground and appeared to faint. To this day, possums do the same thing when they are surprised.

POSSUMS

Possums, also called opossums, are common mammals found along the US East Coast, including in the Southeast. Their name comes from the Native American Algonquian languages. The Algonquian word *apasum* means "white animal." Possums pretend to be dead as a defense mechanism. The Cherokee story of the Possum and the Rabbit includes this distinctive behavior.

COMMON CHARACTERS

Native American stories often feature the types of living creatures that the storytellers encountered where they lived. Animals and other parts of the natural world are often seen as having spirits. For some Native Americans, these creatures are like people in that they have a level of consciousness. Rabbits and possums are common animals throughout the Southeastern United States. The Cherokee people would be very familiar with these creatures.

EXPLORE ONLINE

Chapter Four discusses the use of trickster tales by the Cherokee and other Southeastern tribes. The website below explores other trickster stories from the Choctaw tribe. As you know, every source is different. What information does the website give about trickster stories? How do these stories give you more information about the Choctaw tribe?

CHOCTAW STORIES
abdocorelibrary.com/southeast-nations

THE LASTING IMPACT OF ORAL HISTORIES

I n the 1800s, the US government forced most of the Native American tribes in the Southeast to leave their homes and march west to present-day Oklahoma. The tribes that moved to Oklahoma worked to rebuild their communities. They adapted to the new environment with great difficulty. They maintained their tribal governments and reestablished schools. Despite hardships and

The forced westward movement of Native Americans became known as the Trail of Tears.

FORCED TO MOVE WEST

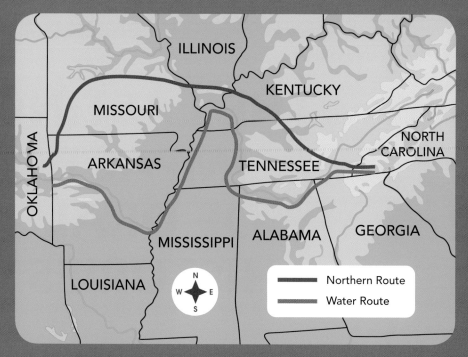

Members of the Cherokee tribe were forced along different routes as they moved west from their homeland to Oklahoma in the 1830s. Some traveled on land, while others traveled over water. What difficulties might travelers have encountered on these routes?

challenges, the Southeastern Nations worked hard to continue their traditional culture.

Today, members of these traditionally Southeastern tribes live in many areas of the country. Some live in tribal communities in the Southeast and Oklahoma. Others live in cities and towns across the United States.

To preserve their culture and traditions, the tribes hold festivals and annual ceremonies. They still play traditional games such as stickball and perform dances. They teach Native languages and history in their own tribal schools.

Oral traditions and storytelling also keep Native American culture and history alive. In addition, some people have begun to write down the stories and traditions of Native American tribes, including those in the Southeast. These written records are another way to preserve the traditions of the Southeastern tribes.

WRITING CHEROKEE STORIES

Sequoyah, a Cherokee man, created a written Cherokee language in 1821. The first Cherokee newspaper was published in 1828.

In 1887, James Mooney began writing down many of the Cherokee oral traditions in English. Mooney was an ethnologist, a person who studies the cultures of different peoples. He spent several years with the Cherokee. He talked with Cherokee elders. They told him many stories, songs, and medicinal plant formulas.

Choctaw storyteller Jon Rice shares stories with school children in 2015.

ORAL TRADITIONS TODAY

Like many Native American tribes, the people of the Southeast have an extensive oral history. Their oral traditions include stories, songs, and orations. For centuries, the people of the Southeast passed down their history by word of mouth. Using oral traditions, they recorded the details of important events, daily life, and ceremonies.

Storytelling is still important to the people of the
Southeast. The Cherokee and other tribes still tell oral
histories to entertain and teach morals. They tell stories
to keep their history and culture alive. Storytelling
can also uplift the spirit and strengthen and empower
people. Stella Long is a Choctaw storyteller. She
realized that she wanted to be a storyteller when she
was a patient at a medical clinic in the 1950s. Although
she was terrified of death, Long told stories to people

THE STOMP DANCE

Along with oral traditions, dance tradition continues to be important among the Cherokee and other Southeastern tribes. One important ceremonial tradition is the stomp dance. It is called *stomp* in English because the dancers perform rhythmic steps. The stomp dance is a social and religious dance. It is often performed as part of the annual Green Corn Ceremony. During the dance, participants sing in a call-and-response format, with a leader calling out a song and a chorus of men responding. The stomp dance can include hundreds of participants.

who were dying. Her words helped them feel at peace. Today, Long tells stories to help people heal in many ways. She ends each story with a Choctaw healing song.

The stories told today have been passed down from generation to generation. These stories maintain a connection with peoples' ancestors. They help people today learn more about the beliefs and cultures of the Cherokee people and other Southeastern Nations.

STRAIGHT TO THE
SOURCE

Cherokee silversmith Sequoyah created a written Cherokee language in the 1820s. Missionary Elias Boudinot described this development, and its use with a printing press, in May 1826:

> The Cherokees have thought it advisable that there should be established, a Printing Press and a Seminary of respectable character; and for these purposes your aid and patronage are now solicited. They wish the types, as expressed in their resolution, to be composed of English letters and Cherokee characters. Those characters have now become extensively used in the nation; their religious songs are written in them; there is an astonishing eagerness in people of all classes and ages to acquire a knowledge of them; and the New Testament has been translated into their language. All this impresses on them the immediate necessity of procuring types.

> Source: Elias Boudinot. "An Address." *Southeastern Native American Documents, 1730–1842*. University of Georgia, n.d. Web. Accessed January 6, 2017.

What's the Big Idea?

Take a close look at Boudinot's words. What is his main idea? What evidence does he use to support this idea?

STORY
SUMMARIES

Grandmother Spider Steals the Fire (Choctaw)

In the beginning, the world is dark. Grandmother Spider volunteers to steal fire from people in the east. She spins a web to the east and brings a clay container to hold the fire. When Grandmother Spider brings the fire back, the animals, birds, and insects are afraid of it. She teaches humans how to keep the fire burning and safe.

The Origin of Corn (Natchez)

While spying on the Corn Woman, two girls see how she fills baskets of corn and beans by rubbing and shaking her body. When the girls refuse to eat the food, the Corn Woman warns that they will have to get their own food. She instructs the girls to burn her body and spread the ashes on the ground. The next summer, corn, beans, and pumpkins grow where the ashes were spread.

Why the Possum's Tail Is Bare (Cherokee)

When Possum brags about his long, bushy tail, Rabbit decides to play a trick on him. He invites Possum to a dance and sends Cricket to style his tail. Possum does not realize Cricket is cutting off his tail's hair. At the dance, the animals shout and laugh. Possum sees that his tail is bare. He is so embarrassed that he falls over on the ground and appears to faint.

STOP AND
THINK

Say What?

Find five words in this book that you are unfamiliar with. Find each word in the glossary or a dictionary. Rewrite each word's definition in your own words. Then use each word in a sentence.

Why Do I Care?

Native American oral histories have links to spirituality. What kinds of stories with spiritual links have you heard in your own community? Have you heard such stories elsewhere, such as on television or in movies? What purposes do these stories serve?

Surprise Me

Think about what you learned from this book. What two or three facts did you find most surprising? Write a short paragraph about each, describing what you found surprising and why.

Take a Stand

This book discusses oral traditions of the Southeastern Native American tribes. Take a position on the benefits of storytelling traditions as compared to written stories, and write a short essay detailing your opinion, reasons for your opinion, and facts and details that support those reasons.

GLOSSARY

ceremony
a religious event
or observance

climate
the typical weather
conditions of a place or
region over time

crop
a plant that is harvested for
food, clothing, or other uses

culture
the shared ways of life and
beliefs of a group of people

generation
a group of people born and
living around the same time

hoe
a long-handled gardening
tool with a thin metal blade
used to break up soil

oral traditions
stories, songs, and speeches
that are passed from
generation to generation by
word of mouth

oration
a formal speech

sacred
something that is holy
or having to do with
spiritual beliefs

thatched
covered with straw or
similar material

tribe
a group of Native Americans
who share a culture

LEARN
MORE

Books

Gray-Kanatiiosh, Barbara A. *Chickasaw*. Minneapolis, MN: Abdo Publishing, 2007.

Powell, Marie. *Traditional Stories of the Plains Nations*. Minneapolis, MN: Abdo Publishing, 2018.

Rea, Amy C. *The Trail of Tears*. Minneapolis, MN: Abdo Publishing, 2016.

Websites

To learn more about Native American Oral Histories, visit **abdobooklinks.com**. These links are routinely monitored and updated to provide the most current information available.

Visit **abdocorelibrary.com** for free additional tools for teachers and students.

INDEX

Braveboy-Locklear,
  Barbara, 13

Cherokee, 6, 8, 9, 27,
  29, 32, 33, 36, 37,
  39–41
Chickasaw, 6
chickees, 9
Choctaw, 6, 8, 15,
  19–21, 31, 33, 39,
  40
corn, 5, 21, 23–27, 40
Corn Woman, 24–26
creation stories, 11,
  15, 21
Creek, 6, 8, 9

fire, 5, 15–19, 20, 27

Grandmother Spider,
  15–20
Green Corn
  Ceremony, 27, 40

Indian Removal Act, 9

Long, Stella, 39–40
Lumbee, 8, 13

mound building, 24

Natchez, 6, 23, 24,
  26–27

Possum, 30–33
pottery, 19, 20, 21

Rabbit, 29–33

Seminole, 6, 9
Sequoyah, 37, 41
Southeastern region,
  6–8
stomp dance, 40

tobacco, 27
Trail of Tears, 9, 35–36
tricksters, 29–33

villages, 5, 6, 9–10

About the Author

Carla Mooney is the author of several books for young readers. She lives in Pittsburgh, Pennsylvania, with her husband and three children.